Air Show!

LARRY ROGERS

Acknowledgements

Thank you to my son, Bryan, for your inspiration and design guidance.

Print Books by Larry Rogers

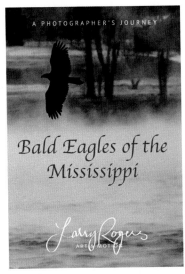

Bald Eagles of the Mississippi

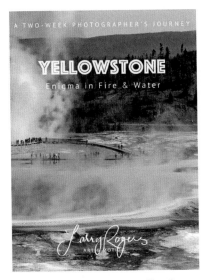

Yellowstone: Enignma in Fire & Water

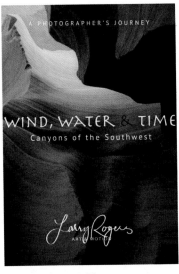

Wind, Water & Time

eBooks by Larry Rogers

Getting the Shot: Yellowstone

Getting the Shot: Death Valley

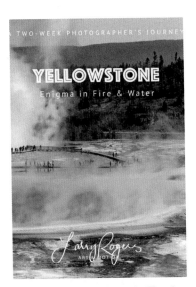

Yellowstone: Enignma in Fire & Water

*T*he desire to fly is an idea handed down to us by our ancestors who... looked enviously on the birds soaring freely through space... on the infinite highway of the air.

Wilbur Wright

INSIDE >

INTRODUCTION

First Powered Flight

At 10:35 am on Wednesday, December 17, 1903, the age of powered flight began. Two brothers, owners of a bicycle shop in Dayton, Ohio, shared a lifelong passion for flight and would become famous for inventing and building the first machine capable of taking flight under the control of a human pilot.

It would not be long before the amazing news that man could really fly would explode around the world. And, of course, people would travel near and far for a glimpse of an early 'flying machine' leaving the ground and returning safely. There must have been an untold number of such gatherings in those early days of the early 1900's, and the case can be made that these were the first air shows.

Next came the 'Barnstormers,' fearless early fliers who put on brave performances in front of small, circus-like crowds across the United States and the world.

In this book I have made the assumption that readers are interested in learning about today's 'organized' air shows, those which attract the best aircraft to be on display and the best performers to demonstrate in the air. So, based upon that assumption, let's learn a bit of history about organized air shows.

History of Air Shows

The year 1909 witnessed a number of large gatherings around the world that were centered around the new technology of flight and those brave men who piloted the machines. The first ocurred on July 10, 1909, and was called the 'Internationale Luftschiffahrt-Ausstellung,' held in Frankfurt Germany. A month later, in August 1909, the first truly international gathering occurred in Reims, France.

Early air shows were affairs with great flair, much like Formula 1 auto races, or the World Cup in soccer, or the Olympics. Pilots and manufacturers would put on displays of skill and daring to out-perform their rivals in the industry.

Political unrest and two world wars took the world stage between 1914 and 1945. Though great progress was made in terms of avaiation design and manufacturing, much of the new technology was held close to the vest in the interest of national security during wartime.

The world waited until the post-World War II late 1940's for a glimpse of the machines that had battled for supremacy in foreign lands and won the Great War and Second Great War that followed.

Warbirds on Display and in the Air

In 1946, the US Navy/Marine Corps Blue Angels aerial flight demonstration team was formed and toured bases across the United States. America was hungry for a glimpse of the machines that had won the war and brought peace back to the world. In 1947, the United States Air Force was split off from the US Army, then known as the Army Air Corps.

A few years later, in 1953, the US Air Force Thunderbirds were formed and demonstrated in front of crowds across America.

Today, larger air shows like those held in Dayton, Ohio, Chicago, Illinois, and military bases around the country, will feature 'static' displays of historic military aircraft spanning the entire history of powered flight, from a working replica of the Wright Flyer, to the B-17 named 'Memphis Belle,' to the now-famous F4-U Corsair of 'Baa Baa Black Sheep' fame. Many of these legacy planes are still maintained in flight-ready condition by volunteer organizations with a passion for preserving the heritage of the planes and people that saved the world.

A wonderful example of the people who saved the world has been on the schedule recently at a number of air shows around the country - The Tuskegee Airmen, or 'Red Tails.' I encourage the reader to learn more about this African American flight unit and the planes they flew in World War II combat for our country.

See the 'Photo Tour' section of the this book for many of my personal favorite photos of warbirds and early flying machines, as well as some of the most cutting-edge technology, including the B-2 Stealth Bomber and F-22 Raptor.

Stunning and Breathtaking Aerial Demonstrations

I attended my first air show during the summer of 1974 at Ramstein Air Force Base, Germany. I was stationed near Ramstein between the fall of 1973 and the summer of 1976. Living near a major military base in an overseas troop deployment area is unlike anything I have experienced since.

On a typical day I would see at least one C5-A Galaxy super transport plane approaching at low altitude, then departing a few hours later. Exotic fighter planes of that era were also a common sight, coming and going at all hours of the day and night.

I'm glad my first air show was the Ramstein Air Show. Because of its location, there was an international flair. The Air Force (in those days) opened the gates to the base to local German nationals who wanted to see the base, the static displays of American firepower, and of course, the aerial demonstrations. There were vendors selling food and drink, as well as souvenirs. The main aerial performance team at my first air show was the Royal Air Force Red Arrows from the UK, and I was instantly hooked on the speed, agility, and yes, the sound. The booming and bone-rattling sound vibrated my clothes as the Red Arrows flew low overhead.

Today, major air shows such my 'local' air show in Dayton, Ohio, will typically feature one of the two US military demonstration teams, the Navy/Marine Corps Blue Angels or the Air Force Thunderbirds, along with civil and military demonstrations of individual aircraft. In alternating years, the Dayton Air Show will also feature a re-enactment team called Tora! Tora! Tora! which includes ground-based pyrotechnics to simulate explosions from bombs dropped by Japanese planes during the WWII Battle of Midway.

What to Expect, How to Dress, and How to Photograph an Air Show

My number one advice is to expect large crowds, both on the highway and on the ground. Plan accordingly, don't even think of bringing pets, and think long and hard before bringing small children. In addition to all the issues of a large crowd, the sound overhead will be deafening at times. Be sure to pack enough ear plugs for everyone in your group.

My number two advice is to pay attention to the weather forecast when planning your trip. I don't know the scientific explanation, but air show locations are the coldest places on earth in cool seasons and the hottest places on earth rest of the time. Dress accordingly. There will be little to no shelter from rain, wind, or sun. Remember, air shows are held on airports, which are places with few buildings, none of which can accomodate thousands of people.

Plan on walking, walking, and walking some more - all day long. Airports that can accomodate large military airplanes offten have runways up to two miles long. To see all of the static displays and vendors, you may have to walk the entire thing, and back, one or more times. Wear comfortable shoes, and socks.

There will likely be nothing to sit or lay on. Take along a lightweight tarp or blanket - waterproof if possible.

Take plenty of water.

Let's talk breifly about photographing an air show. By now, you should know that I will recommed against long, heavy lenses, tripods and camera bags. That stuff is heavy, and anything heavy will be your enemy at an air show...unless... your venue offers a "Photography" ticket package. The Dayton Air Show offers a package called 'Photo Tour and Pit' which includes admission, early access to static displays, and a special reserved location near the flight line with seating and clear access to photograph the performers. The total cost is $80 for the weekend. Regular gate admission starts at 18 per day when purchased at a local Kroger store, or $21 per day at the gate.

I prefer to use a high-resolution (36 MP or higher) DSLR camera with a high frame-rate (8 frames per second, or higher) to capture the action in the sky. Remember to slow down your shutter speed when photographing propeller planes! Still props look goofy on planes in flight.

My personal favorite lens is a 200-400 zoom, which I can hand hold (barely), giving me the ability to shoot directly overhead as well as pan with passing planes. I carry a 1.4x teleconverter in my pocket, but often that ends up being too much lens for many shots. I much prefer to get my shots easily in-frame, rather than having planes going out of frame at a critical time.

Don't mess with polarizing filters - they are hightly directional and may produce erratic results as you pan with moving planes. Last, take every data card you own. Data cards are so light you won't even know they qre in your pack.

Wright Flyer Replica

The Dayton Air Show traditionally features legacy flight demonstrations. Dayton, Ohio, is the home of the Wright Brothers and it was no surprise to see this working replica flown both days at the 2010 air show.

Tech Tip: Propeller-driven aircraft such as the Wright Flyer are more difficult to photograph than jet performers. You don't want to 'freeze' the propellers. Some motion blur makes your photos look realistic. Start at a shutter speed of 1/60 second, but closely examine your photos to ensure sharpness throught the frame. Increase shutter speed slightly as needed to get a sharp image of the plane and a bit of prop blur.

WRIGHT FLYER

DAYTON OH (2010)

Prep Tip: Photographing propeller-driven airplanes is challenging. A great photo requires slowing down the shutter to 1/125 sec or slower, while manually panning with the movement of the plane. Practice this technique at a local airport in advance.

Tech Tip: If your airshow event schedule shows performer practice sessions early in the day, use this time to take practice shots. Each airplane engine is different and each performance requires different prop speeds. Make a note of the best settings.

AT-6 TEXAN

DAYTON OH (2010)

Story of the Memphis Belle

The original Memphis Belle was built by Boeing Aircraft Company and delivered to the United States Army Air Corps in July 1942. The US Army Air Corps became the US Air Force in 1947.

The plane in the photo on this page is a true B-17, but not the original Memphis Belle. This replica plane saw combat duty in World War II, but it has been repainted with the appropriate unit insignia and nose art that were flown on the Memphis Belle for the 1990 movie. The replica now tours the country, offering a chance to experience flight aboard a true classic warbird.

The original Memphis Belle now resides at the United States Air Force Museum in Dayton, Ohio. The plane was first placed in a restoration hangar at Wright-Patterson Air Force Base in Dayton in 2005. Restoration was completed in 2018, when the move to the Air Force Museum was completed.

B-17 FLYING FORTRESS

DAYTON OH (2010)

Tips for Photographing Propeller-driven Planes in Flight

My most important advice for anyone photographing propeller-driven planes in flight is to remember to slow down your shutter speed to create a bit of propeller blur. Stopped propellers (from high shutter speeds) will make your photos appear to be 'model' aircraft.

Basic photo tips for any planes-in-flight are similar to many other photographic situations: pay attention to light direction. Light on this photo reflected off the plane toward me, pleasantly illuminating the fuselage of the plane; take as many photos as you can, and look for compositions like this, in which the front, sides, and tail are visible.

P-51 MUSTANG
DAYTON OH (2012)

North American P-51D Mustang, "Quick Silver"

This beautifully restored warbird is the result of decades of work by the late William 'Bill' Yoak. It is flown at air shows around the USA by Bill's son Scott.

North American Aviation manufactured the plane in 1945, at which time it was placed into service. Following years of military service and restoration work, the new 'Quick Silver' took its first flight in April, 2007.

F4-U CORSAIR
DAYTON OH (2014)

Static Displays

Almost every air show I have attended has offered access to 'static' displays - real aircraft that were flown into the show and then staged in an area where visitors can get up close. Quite often there will also be a crew member available to meet visitors and respond to questions about the aircraft.

Special Access Tickets

Special access to static displays may be available, although sometimes at an extra cost. The Dayton, Ohio, air show offers a ticket package that includes parking in a reserved media area, access to a reserved seating area near mid-field with a covered area and cold water, and early access to static displays before the venue opens to the public. Early access does mean you must be there on time at 7:00 am.

These special access tickets are a bit pricey, but may be worth the cost for anyone who wants to get really great photos of static displays with minimal interference from other visitors as well as a premium location to photograph aerial performances.

Location, Location, Location

All aerial demostration teams and solo performers at air shows make use of ground references during their performances. They typically practice their show choreography at least once prior to the actual show. This becomes important to anyone wanting to get the best possible photos of the performers, because the choreography of their performances will be based on a single location on the field. Usually that location will be 'show center,' roughly the center point in front of the spectator viewing area.

A good tip for locating 'show center' is to look for an announcer stand - the place where the show announcers are set up with sound equipment to narrate the show and make make public service announcements.

Photographer Etiquette in a Crowded Place

It may sound ridiculous at first, but working photographers actually have 'rules of behavior' that I will share here - just so you will know what to expect when sharing a crowded space with them.

One very basic behavior of working photographers is the belief that everyone has a right to get their shot, but no right to do so in a way that impedes the shot of another person. This means that one should first look around to see who else may be setting up near you, then find a place to stand where you will not impede the shot of another. Take your shot, then move on so that others may have their opportunity to get a shot, too.

Setting up a tripod can be a touchy topic, especially in crowded places. Most air shows will allow them, but please never set up a tripod unless you are in a reserved area for photographers, or there is plenty of space to pass.

Packing your Photo Gear for the Show

Depending upon the particular venue of the show, you should anticipate a lot of walking, so much walking that the thought of returning to your car or truck for a sandwich or a lens you forgot to put in your pack is just too traumatic.

So, here are my tips on gear choices for your first air show. I'll assume that gear choice doesn't matter for iPad or smartphone photographers, and give recommendations for the rest of you who plan to take along a camera with inter-changeable lenses (either DSLR or mirrorless).

My first recommendation is to take along a DSLR if you have one. Today's mirrorless cameras with digital viewfinder all suffer from somewhat slower playbnack through the viewfinder compared with the instantaneous view through a DSLR. This will be important when shooting bursts as planes perform maneuvers. My next, and last, recommendation is to choose a zoom lens with a range that supports near and long shots, such as a 100-400 mm zoom.

TUSKEGEE AIRMEN
DAYTON OH (2018)

Story of the "Red Tails"

The 99th Fighter Squadron was the first African-American flying squadron in World War II, and the first to deploy overseas (to North Africa), in April 1943. Although the squadron trained and deployed with other aircraft, including the P-40 Warhawk, the plane with which the group is most identified is the North American P-51B and D models.

The red markings that distinguished the squadron included the tail, rudder and prop spinner. The unit also traditionally painted yellow wing bands on their planes.

65 Years Young (and counting)

The Boeing B-52 bomber was placed into service with the the US Air Force in 1955, and it has been in service continuously since. Even though more advanced aircraft have been introduced in recent years, the Air Force may continue to utilize B-52s through 2050. A total of 744 B-52s were produced between 1952 and 1963.

As far as I know, the B-52 holds the record for longest continuous service among all aircraft ever used by any US military department.

The aircraft shown in this photo from a 2009 air show is the 'H' model. The B-52H is the last in a long line of models. A total of 102 'H' models were produced between 1961 and 1963 to support the Vietnam War. A total 78 B-52s are still in service today.

B-52 STRATOFORTRESS

DAYTON OH (2009)

Vietnam War Workhorse, Still in Service after 60 years

McDonnell-Douglas began production of the first F-4 Phantoms prior to 1960, when it was placed into service with the US Navy. Later, it was adopted by the US Marine Corps and US Air Force.

The F-4 is the only aircraft to be flown by both the US Navy Blue Angels and US Air Force Thunderbirds aerial demonstration teams.

The F-4 was retired from US service in 1996, following air support service in the Gulf War (1991-1996). It remains in service in other nations, including Japan, South Korea, Greece and Turkey.

F-4 PHANTOM II
DAYTON OH (2012)

UH-1 HUEY
DAYTON OH (2009)

AH-64 APACHE
DAYTON OH (2009)

US ARMY GOLDEN KNIGHTS
DAYTON OH (2018)

Today's High Tech Stealth Fighter

The Lockheed Martin/Boeing F-22A Raptor is US Air Force's air superiority stealth fighter. It also has capabilities for ground attack, electronic warfare and signal intelligence.

This airplane is a lot of fun to watch and photograph. Watch for canopy starburst reflections, as in this image, as well as compression vapor and afterburner flares as shown on the next two pages.

Don't forget to put your earplugs in!

Prep Tip: Photographing the F-22 is a blast, literally. This aircraft produces a painful sound level as it passes by. I highly recommend taking earplugs to the air show, and using them! I think I could feel my clothes vibrating as it flew by!

Tech Tip: The canopy of the F-22 is a highly reflective gold metallic color that may produce a starburst effect. To capture the starburst effect, as I did in this image, use a small aperture (f16 or smaller) and compensate with ISO if necessary.

F-22 RAPTOR
DAYTON OH (2018)

C-17 GLOBEMASTER III

DAYTON OH (2018)

Today's Military Transport Workhorse

The McDonnell-Douglas/Boeing C-17 Globemaster III US Air Force's worldwide military transport plane. The original development was done by McDonnell-Douglas in the 1980s through the early 1990s. McDonnell-Douglas merged with Boeing in 1997, after which Boeing continued to manufacture the planes for export partners after completion of deliveries to the US Air Force.

C-17 missions include strategic airlift, troop and cargo transport, medical evacuation and air drop.

The last C17 delivery was completed in November 2015.

B-2 SPIRIT
DAYTON OH (2009)

F-18 SUPERHORNET
DAYTON OH (2010)

A-10 WARTHOG
DAYTON OH (2009)

USAF THUNDERBIRDS
DAYTON OH (2009)

US NAVY BLUE ANGE[LS]

DAYTON OH (2018)

US Navy Blue Angels: What to Expect

Each air show venue presents a unique set of opportunities and limitations with respect to the actual aerial demonstration a team can perform there. In addition to that, weather is the final determinant of the maneuvers the team will perform on any given day.

If you have not seen the Blue Angels perform, but you are planning to see them soon, I recommend a visit to the official website, _blueangels.navy.mil_. Read up on the team members, the show maneuvers, the schedule, etc. Also, you may find sites online with videos of a complete show from the current season. Advance research will prepare you for each photo opportunity during a show.

As soon as the team takes off, you will notice that they separate into two sub-teams: The 'Diamond,' which includes planes 1 through 4, and the 'Opposing Solos,' planes 5 and 6. On rare occasions you may see plane 7 used in a show in place of one of the other planes. Plane 7 is a two-seater that is flown by the narrator and used to take local dignitaries for rides during the practice day(s) prior to a show. At times during a show, all six planes will fly together in a 'Delta' formation.

Personally, I like to keep an eye on both of the sub-teams and I have learned to watch for certain situations which almost always lead up to a great photography shot. One situation involves the opposing solos, as they approach the airfield from opposite ends. This almost always means a low altitude head-on pass. I have a tip for those who will have a camera

capable of shooting bursts at a rate of at least 6 frames per second (use the the fastest frame rate your camera supports). Set the camera to 'continuous high' shooting mode and the autofocus mode to continuous servo mode (AF-C for Nikon). As the planes reach opposite ends of airfield choose one of them to follow through the viewfinder on your camera. Track that plane in the viewfinder until it gets close to the center of the field, then press and hold the shutter until you see the other plane flash by as you watch through the viewfinder. Hopefully you have captured a great shot of the head-on pass. The opposing solos will actually spend most of the show repeating this maeuver, so you will have a number of chances to get it.

The Diamond and the Delta formations can also present opportunities for great shots. I watch for these formations to get low and parallel to the ground as they approach from far off the airfield - this usually ends with all planes bursting away from the group.

Lastly, the group formations themselves make pretty nice photos.

Artistically, I find that the dark blue color of the planes looks very interesting against a blue sky with a few white puffy clouds, but I don't get too selective while shooting. I leave my camera set on coninuous-high burst mode so that I get several versions of each shot to choose from in post-processing.

My current camera body of choice for air shows is the Nikon D850, and my lens of choice is the Nikon 200-400 f/4 zoom. The camera you use is the least important thing - get a good spot to stand near mid-field and enjoy the show!

Beyond the Click

An Invitation

I hope you have enjoyed reading 'Air Show!' I invite you to think about what comes next.

Will you seek out experiences similar to the air show experiences I shared? Many experiences like this can be found near home. To find air shows near you, a great place to start is the home page of the US Navy Blue Angels (*blueangels.navy.mil*) or US Air Force Thunderbirds (*afthunderbirds.com*). If so, will you use any of the planning or photo tips in this publication? I hope you will! In preparation for that, I have a few final thoughts.

Artist, explorer, or both?

I invite you to consider how you want to experience your next exploration or adventure. There is no right or wrong way to experience an air show, but there are very different experiences to be had. I, for example, consider myself an 'artist' whose brush is a camera, whose paint is a computer and software, and whose canvas is the print media upon which my visual art will be seen and, I hope, enjoyed by others.

I am also an 'explorer.' In fact, I was an explorer before I became an artist, as I traveled abroad for military service as a young man. That experience opened my mind to the realization that the world is a larger and even more wonderful collection of experiences than I had previously imagined. These experiences are available for everyone to enjoy. Tragically, too few of us actually have these experiences, for a variety of reasons.

My "why," the reasons I explore and share

I explore and share my experiences so that other people might be inspired to do things and see places they may not otherwise do and see. A few of those people who are inspired to see and enjoy new things and places may even become future stewards, which is a vision that inspires me to embark on even more adventures and share them with others, like you.

The medium I have chosen for sharing my message is the printed word, illustrated with works of art that I generate from a digital camera and illustrate on the printed page or, in some cases, on exquisite fine art paper or special metal print surfaces. With that said, it would be a disservice to you, the reader, if I stopped with that over-simplified description. In the interest of fairness and full disclosure, there is much more to the story of how these images are made.

Before and after the click

It is absolutely true that this publication shares the images from several years of attending air shows near my home in southwest Ohio, but the truth is, I have made many visits to air shows, national parks, and other places of interest. Before each outing, I begin planning the specific shots (planes and maneuvers, in this case) about three months prior to the trip. I start my planning for air shows with a visit to the website of the show itself, where I learn about the scheduled performers. From there, I visit the website of each team or performer to learn about them and see examples of photos they like well enough to place on their website. This gives me a head start on setting up for the day of the show.

All of this starts before the first click of the camera, and there is much processing of my images after the last click. Mose of the work is before and after the click.

To the Artist: The click is only the beginning

Communication is the artist's objective. My objective is to share the feeling I had when I stood at a place. I never have forgotten the sensory experience of a place that moved me - the height of the mountains, the smell of the pines, the sound of the wind in the trees or the roar of a nearby river.

For my fellow photographers desiring to make a stronger connection with your audience, in my experience communication through imagery is not a function of technical perfection. Sharpness, saturation and contrast are not as important as your composition and imact of the scene. I like to visit some places over and over, and I try to get images that evoke different emotional reactions, like clear skies with white puffy clouds as well as angry, stormy skies, or even the lucky rainbow just as a shower passes and the sun returns. Each of these images will evoke different reactions in the viewer.

Art is about emotion

All images shown in this publication have been processed using software that enables me to 'shape' the image in such a way that it helps me recall how I felt when I captured it. I often think back to a time when I was first learning digital photography. I would go someplace hoping to get stunning images like those I saw online or in photo books, but I failed every time, because I had not yet become an artist.

Before I share images in print, I process them in a way that will evoke emotion in my reader. My tips are intended to be helpful, but the truth is, most people will not have invested the time and expense that I have. Just know that your images are your own - you were there!

Forever a student

Anyone willing to take the artist's journey can match or exceed the image 'quality' seen in this or any other publication. Yes, you can! Let me share a few tips to get your started on your journey:

Be forever a student

> Study everything about your subjects
> Ask questions
> Listen to what others have to say
> Share
> Experiment

Learn what "style" is, and develop yours

Know "why" you make art and commit to it

Be disciplined

Question everything you do

Make good art, and only good art

Closing thoughts

I have shared this story in the hope that you will be inspired get outside and have your own experiences. Your experience will be yours to remember. Some of you may want to share your experiences, and I hope I have given that group some ideas and inspiration to inspire others.

Larry Rogers

About the Author

Larry Rogers has been photographing Americana, air shows, national parks and wildlife for more than 40 years. Formally educated in electrical engineering and computer science, Larry was given his first camera around age 8 and cannot recall a time when he did not have a camera.

Following graduation from college, he served as an Air Defense Officer in the US Army, a US government civilian employee and small business owner. But, throughout, his passion for wildlife, wild places, and the environment fueled his love of photography and the arts.

With a burning passion to constantly learn and develop his art to a high level, Larry is now extending his art to new perspectives, flying a drone and publishing books which he hopes will inspire the next generation of conservation and nature photographers.

He currently lives in southwest Ohio, in the United States. He is the father of two sons, and grandfather to two granddaughters.

Larry welcomes readers to follow and/or contact him via social media, email or comments on his website.

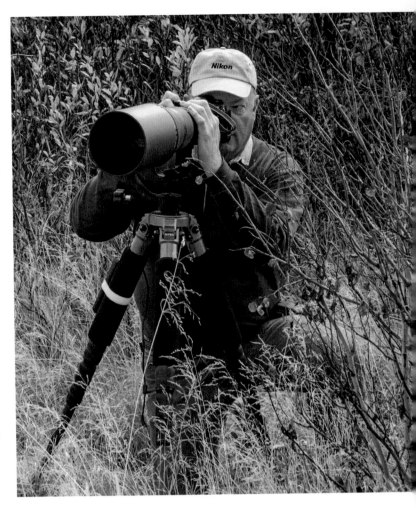

Contact

Instagram: larryrogersartandmotion
LinkedIn: linkedin.com/in/the-conservancy-project
email: inquire@larryrogers.us
Twitter: @larryrogers
Website: larryrogersphotography.us

Follow us on Instagram for up-to-date information on new products and current projects.

More from Larry Rogers

eBooks are available in the iBooks Store
Getting the Shot: Yellowstone
Getting the Shot: Death Valley

Art prints are available at larryrogersphotography.us

Americana
Air Shows
Yellowstone Landscapes
Yellowstone Wildlife
Grand Teton National Park
and many more galleries

Be safe in your travels, and remember, "Take only photographs, and leave only footprints!"

Made in the USA
Lexington, KY
19 November 2019